A Very Young Reaper

Written and Illustrated by
Winslow J. Furber

AuthorHouse™
1663 Liberty Drive
Bloomington, IN 47403
www.authorhouse.com
Phone: 1 (800) 839-8640

Published by AuthorHouse: 10/31/2017

ISBN: 978-1-5462-1532-5 (sc)
ISBN: 978-1-5462-1531-8 (e)

Library of Congress Control Number: 2017916940

Print information available on the last page.

This book is printed on acid-free paper.

authorHOUSE®

Tim Reaper was born without any hair

But he was a happy baby
with fine healthy bones

Which was all that mattered to his parents Kim and Grim

And hide—and—go—seek

His parents worked
hard and shared the
household chores

Tim was sometimes bored
without Kim and Grim

One day Tim looked out the window

Tim wanted to go outside, but his mom said "No". She told him it was hard for others to understand and accept the Reapers

But one day Tim snuck outside when his parents were busy

Tim marveled at the beauty
of all the living things

And he loved feeling the
wind tickle his bones

Kim found Tim crying

That night Grim and
Kim told Tim about
the sadness and
wonder of Death

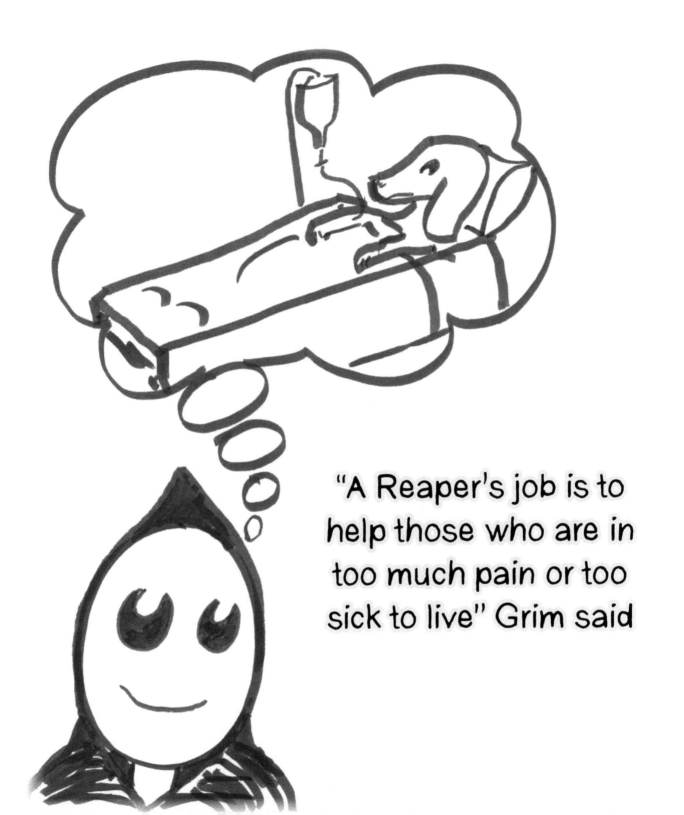

"A Reaper's job is to help those who are in too much pain or too sick to live" Grim said

After talking to his parents, Tim understood a little better

As his spirits improved, Tim started going outside again

But he was careful to only step on rocks

Sometimes he made the rocks
into paths he could walk

And he smelled the
flowers and the trees
But was careful not to touch

And the wind still
tickled his bones

One day Tim came
across a porcupine who
was very old and sick

The porcupine
told Tim all about
his wonderful life
And all that
he had seen
and done

Then the porcupine asked Tim for the one thing he had never had

CPSIA information can be obtained
at www.ICGtesting.com
Printed in the USA
BVHW021721151118
533051BV00002B/3/P